Dear Parents/Teachers:

Yay! Your child/student is interest in learning t(
The goal: reading on their own and loving it!

MW00940638

Waldorf Readers are designed to help your child/student enjoy the learning process. Our Readers have 4 levels to guide your child/student to independent reading.

Each level collection has interesting stories, unique characters and colorful illustrations. All Waldorf Readers are original works with characters your child/student will enjoy. Waldorf Publishing strives to accommodate a full reading experience for any child/student at any reading level.

Waldorf Readers will entertain your child/student level by level.

Spark Reading **Preschool-Kindergarten**
-Large font and easy words
-Illustrations to accompany the storyline
-No more than two syllables

Level 1 Waldorf Readers introduce children/students to reading. Sentences are short and simple. Using phonics skills, children/students will sound out words.

Read Together **Preschool-Grade 1**
-Short sentences
-Easy to understand stories
-Simple vocabulary
-No more than two syllables

Level 2 Waldorf Readers keep the excitement for reading strong. Sentences will include bigger words and more in depth story lines, which are sure to entertain.

Independent Reading **Grade 1-3**
-Exciting and relatable characters
-Plots and story lines that are relatable and easy to follow
-Topics children enjoy
-No more than 3 syllable words

Level 3 Waldorf Readers have larger paragraphs and words that will challenge and engage children/students.

Advanced Independent Reading **Grade 2-4**
-In depth plot and story lines
-Larger blocks of text
-Full color illustration
-Words with 3+ syllables

Level 4 Waldorf Readers are more challenging and lengthy. These books are perfect for children/students who want to read longer books and still enjoy colorful illustrations. Level 4 Waldorf Readers are the last level before advancing to Waldorf Chapter Books.

Published by Waldorf Publishing
2140 Hall Johnson Road
#102-345
Grapevine, Texas 76051
www.WaldorfPublishing.com

Belle and Cayenne Visit the Great State of Montana

ISBN: 978-1-64764-881-7

Library of Congress Control Number: 2020937043

Copyright © 2020

All rights reserved. No part of this book may be reproduced or transmitted in any form or by any means whatsoever without express written permission from the author, except in the case of brief quotations embodied in critical articles and reviews. Please refer all pertinent questions to the publisher. All rights reserved. No part of this book may be reproduced or transmitted in any form or by any means, electronic or mechanical, including photocopying, recording, or by an information storage and retrieval system except by a reviewer who may quote brief passages in a review to be printed in a magazine or newspaper without permission in writing from the publisher.

Illustrations by Ashley Kenny
Design by Baris Celik

Belle and Cayenne Visit the Great State of Montana

WALDORF PUBLISHING

Meet the Chillin' Chilis! Belle and Cayenne are a couple of carefree and curious Capsicum peppers.

They are on a voyage to see the United States of America (U.S.A.), a beautiful land and the third largest country in the world

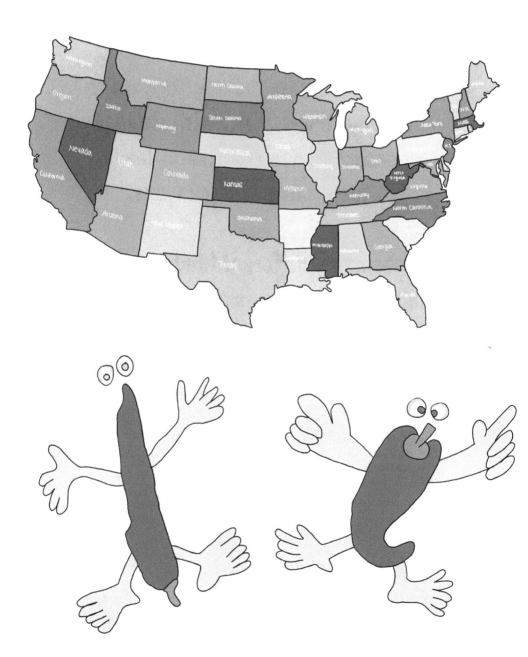

The chilies are looking forward to visiting the U.S.A., with its many deserts, beaches, rivers, lakes, mountains, and canyons.

It has many different kinds of flowers and trees, and birds and animals, and crops.

There are a whopping 300 million people living in the U.S.A., across a wide range of cultures!

But these serene sisters have a tendency to get separated! As Belle searches for Cayenne, she will discover the great state of Montana.

Belle encounters fun new places while exploring "The Treasure State." She visits her friend, Helena, who is named after the state's capital.

The rugged and ruddy chilis, Belle
and Cayenne, are on a new adventure,
exploring the western part of the United
States.

The peppers plan to hike through
the state of Montana in the Rocky
Mountains.

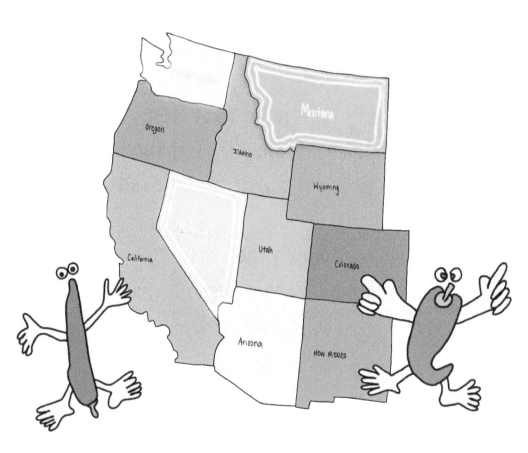

As they then head west towards the Pacific coast, they'll visit the warm southwestern state of Nevada.

They will finish their trip by visiting the state of Washington, in the Pacific Northwest.

Today, the Chillin' Chilis are visiting the great state of Montana. Will you join them as they discover new places?

"What state is this?" Belle asks Cayenne as she heads for a city in the distance.

Not hearing an answer, Belle turns to her scarlet sibling... only to see that Cayenne is missing!

"This is not good."

She cannot remember when she last saw her, as both had been listening to Salsa music and not paying quite enough attention.

Belle has no choice but to try to find Cayenne along the way.

It's not that they can't get along by themselves, but traveling together is so much fun! Perhaps you can help Belle find Cayenne along the way?

Belle is excited to see her friend, Helena, who lives in Montana. Montana borders the great country of Canada to the north.

Even though the state contains many mountains, such as Montana's tallest, Granite Peak, the eastern part of the state is actually part of the Great Plains.

Helena takes Belle to some interesting cities, including Missoula and Billings.

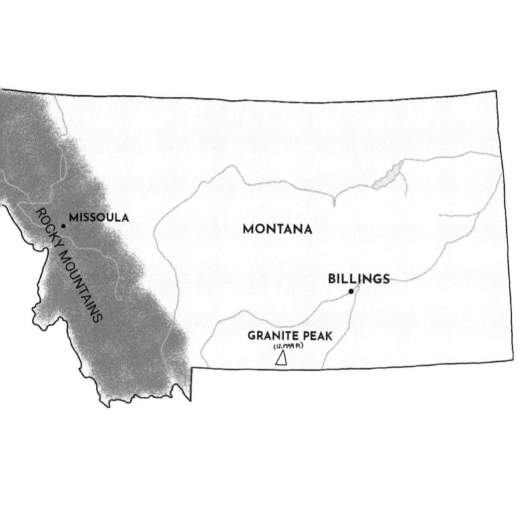

"Have you seen my sister, Helena?" Belle asks. "She's red and usually pretty calm, though a bit spicy if she wants to be."

"I haven't seen her," Helena replies. "Sorry about that!"

Belle knows that Helena helps her parents grow crops and raise livestock on their farm.

Her uncle works in a coal mine, mining for one of the treasures that give Montana its nickname.

The Treasure State

Belle really likes Helena, but she keeps her visits on the short side because Helena always puts poor Belle to work!

Helena tells Belle that Montana's state bird is the Western Meadowlark, the state tree is the Ponderosa Pine, and the state flower is the Bitterroot.

Belle also learns that Montana is the forty-first state to join the U.S.A.

Montana- Number 41 Admitted to USA!

Belle tells Helena that she's thought of a poem during her visit. She asks her to give her opinion after she's finished reciting it:

Helena grew sugar beets, barley, and wheat just east of the Rockies, and near Granite Peak. Her family in Billings sold lumber and wood. Life in Montana was wholesome and good.

"I like that!" Helena said, smiling. She is so proud of the state she lives in and is even prouder after hearing Belle's poem.

Belle finds her state of Montana to be as wonderful as Helena does.

"I'm feeling a bit burned out now,"
a tired Belle decides. "But where is
Cayenne? I've seen all of Montana and
still cannot find her."

Just then she hears some nearby Salsa
music, and turns to see her twin right
behind her, smiling.

"I knew it was feeling hotter than usual in Montana," Helena laughs.

"Well by golly, it's you! Thank goodness." Belle hugs her sister. "Time for a drink of cold water and some rest." Belle yawns and stretches.

Will you meet the chilis on their next adventure?

THE END

CPSIA information can be obtained
at www.ICGtesting.com
Printed in the USA
JSHW041053100221
11758JS00006B/187

9 781647 648817